LIBBY
THE LOBIVIA JAJOIANA

Written by: Regan W. H. Macaulay and Kevin Risk

Illustrated by: Gordon Bagshaw

mirror world publishing

PRINT EDITION

Libby the Lobivia Jajoiana © 2020 by Mirror World Publishing and Regan W. H.
Macaulay, Kevin Risk and Gordon Bagshaw
    Illustrated by: Gordon Bagshaw
    Edited by: Robert Dowsett
    All Rights Reserved.

For more information, contact:
Mirror World Publishing
Windsor, Ontario
www.mirrorworldpublishing.com
info@mirrorworldpublishing.com

ISBN: 978-1-987976-74-8

This inscription is said to be one of many proverbs that can be found sewn in the fabric of Tanzanian kangas. It reads: "education is an ocean". Gordon came across this during his research for the illustration work. He would like to dedicate this book to four brilliant, strong, creative women who have significantly touched his life and been an ocean of education to him: his three sisters, Lori, Karen, and Tracey, and his wife, Raquel.

Kevin and Regan would also like to dedicate this book to all the awesome, strong, inspirational women in their family.

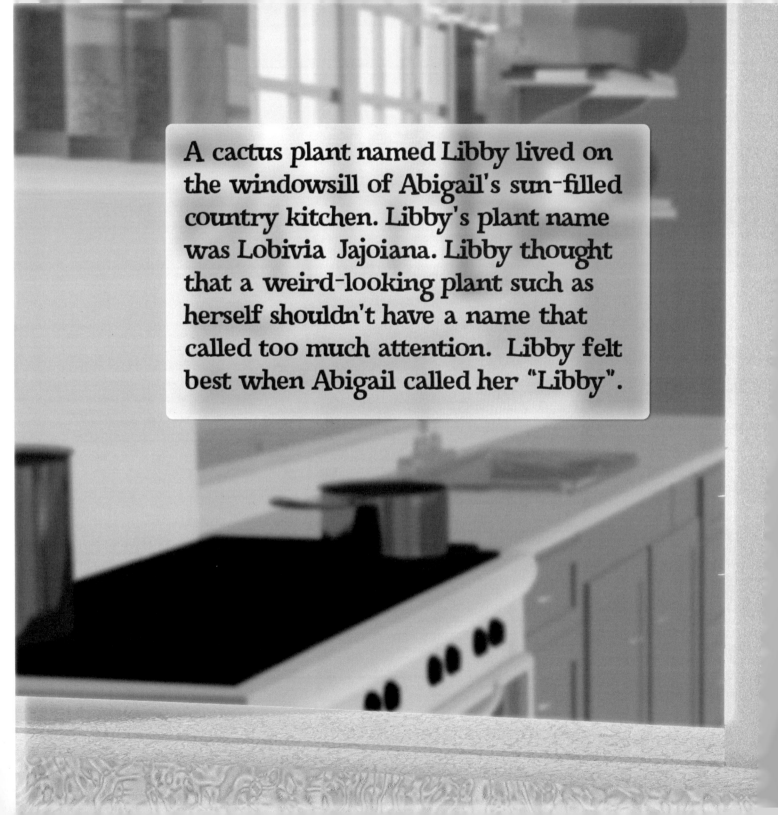

A cactus plant named Libby lived on the windowsill of Abigail's sun-filled country kitchen. Libby's plant name was Lobivia Jajoiana. Libby thought that a weird-looking plant such as herself shouldn't have a name that called too much attention. Libby felt best when Abigail called her "Libby".

The kitchen window overlooked Abigail's garden. The garden was full of all kinds of beautiful plants with pretty leaves and colourful flowers. Not one of them had spiky spines like Libby.

Libby watched Abigail in her garden day after day. Abigail knelt beside each flower and gently turned over its petals in her hands.

Abigail never touches me like that, thought Libby.

One afternoon, Abigail came into the kitchen carrying a package. She put the parcel on the kitchen island. Abigail opened the box.

ELIMU NI BAHARI

Inside was a beautiful plant with leaves like velvet. She placed the plant on the windowsill next to Libby.

"Hello," said the new plant. "I'm an African Violet. What are you? Are you a porcupine?"

"I'm not a porcupine!" replied Libby. "I'm a cactus plant. My name is Libby."

"I thought plants looked like me," said Violet. "How do you like my colourful flowers and big, soft leaves?" She stretched out her blossoms and turned them this way and that, so Libby could see them. "Everyone stops to look at me."

"No one looks at me," said Libby. "Not even Prea, the house cat."

"I don't know what a house cat is, but I'm sure she'll love me," Violet bragged. "I'd like it very much if your prickles don't touch me, okay?"

Violet's request made Libby feel very sad.

That night, Libby heard a clacking sound. She knew it was the sound of Prea's claws against the floor.

Prea bounded up to the windowsill. Prea sniffed Libby and turned away. Prea sniffed Violet. Violet puffed with pride. "She probably wants to kiss me."

Prea's mouth opened showing the tips of her sharp teeth.

"I see you have prickles," said Violet. "Are you a cactus plant, too?"

Prea chomped Violet's flowers. "No!" cried Violet. "Not my beautiful blossoms!"

Abigail ran into the kitchen and shooed Prea away from the windowsill. "Naughty girl," scolded Abigail. Prea raced out of the kitchen.

Abigail gently touched Violet's torn flowers. "You poor thing." Abigail put Violet on a higher shelf. "Now you will be safe and soon get better," Abigail said assuringly.

Violet's blossoms did grow back.

Libby began to grow, too. She grew a
flower—one big, crimson-coloured bloom!

One night, Libby heard a familiar clacking sound on the floor. She knew Prea the cat was coming.

"She's going to eat you," whispered Violet.

Prea jumped up to the sill and sniffed near Libby's flower. She showed her sharp teeth.

Libby trembled. "Please, please don't hurt me."

Prea tried to bite Libby's big red blossom.

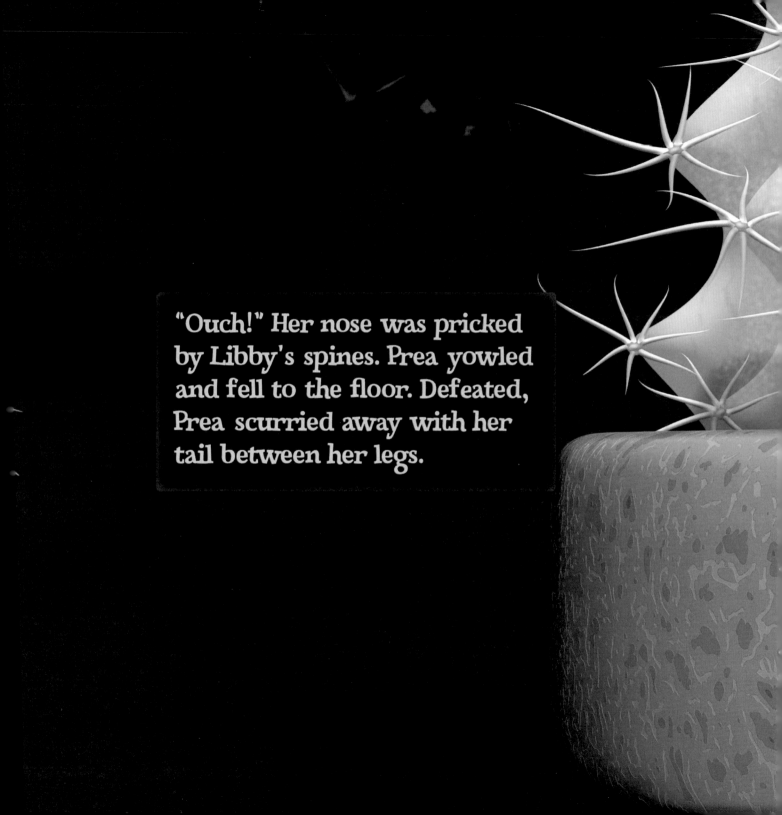

"Ouch!" Her nose was pricked by Libby's spines. Prea yowled and fell to the floor. Defeated, Prea scurried away with her tail between her legs.

Libby heard a small voice coming from beside her. "Your flower is very beautiful," said Violet. "But you know what? I think your needles really make you special. You're lucky you have them."

"Yes," said Libby. "I didn't know how special they made me, until now."

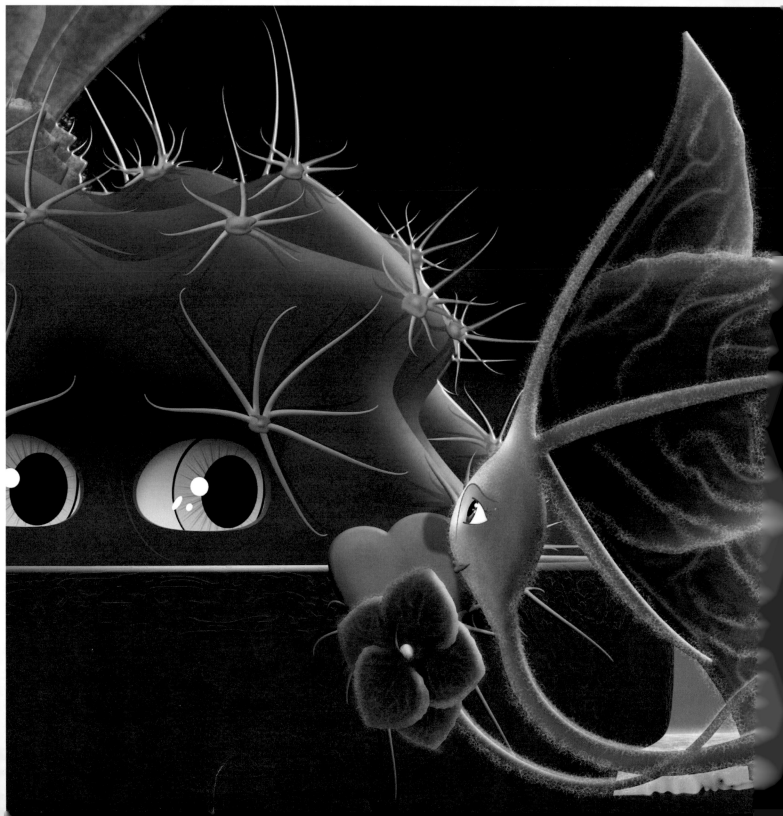

"When we first met, I wasn't very nice to you," Violet admitted. "I'm going to be nicer now that I know you better. Let's be friends."

"Okay," said Libby.

Libby and Violet talked all through the night.

The morning sun came through the window of Abigail's country kitchen. Libby looked at the pretty leaves and colourful flowers of the plants in Abigail's garden. Libby felt proud of her red bloom. She felt especially proud of her spines.

"I've wanted to ask you," said Violet, "is Libby your only name? It's a fine name, but I think a plant as special as you deserves a special name, too."

"Well, I do have a proper Latin name," said Libby. "It's Lobivia Jajoiana."

Violet listened carefully and replied, "I like it. A special, proper name for a special, beautiful friend. Low-BIV-ee-uh Jah-joee-AHN-nuh," Violet repeated.

Libby stretched her needles happily. "Thank you," she answered. "It does suit me."

Acknowledgements

Regan & Kevin

Thank you, Gord, for bringing our story and its characters to life in such a vibrant and nurturing way. We are always on the same page, and we are incredibly grateful for your brilliant energy and creativity.

Mom—our business partner and partner in crime—thank you for your ongoing, vital hard work. Kelsey, adding you to our business team is one of the best things we've ever done!

Mirror World Publishing, as always you have been a delight to work with. Thank you for continuing to believe in our stories.

Thank you to Andrew Petrie for the pronunciation, Dr. Ruth of Hibiscus Publishing, and Lynda of Guardian Angel Publishing for working on the story with us. Thank you to all the readers, young and old, who gave us feedback on "Libby" and to Allan Gardens, Toronto.

Gordon

Regan and Kevin, thank you for inviting me on this creative journey of yours, and for entrusting me with your story artistically. Your patience with the process has not gone unnoticed. This working relationship we have developed together over the years has inspired and challenged me as an artist. Thank you so much for introducing me to Libby.

About the Authors

Regan W. H. Macaulay (left) writes novels, short stories, children's literature, and scripts. Writing is her passion, but she's also a producer and director of theatre, film, and television. She is an animal-enthusiast as well, which led her to become a Certified Canine and Feline Massage Therapist. Other picture storybooks include *Sloth the Lazy Dragon, Tamara Turtle's Life So Far, Mixter Twizzle's Breakfast, Merry Myrrh the Christmas Bat, and Beverlee Beaz the Brown Burmese.* She is also the author of The Trilogy of Horrifically Half-baked Ham, which includes *Space Zombies!* (based on her film, *Space Zombies: 13 Months of Brain-Spinning Mayhem!*—available on iTunes and on DVD), *They Suck*, and *Horror at Terror Creek.*

Kevin Risk (right) has had a varied history. He began in theatre, briefly transitioned into teaching ESL, then settled in library science. He currently works as a media librarian and spends much of his time preoccupied with metadata. When he's not at work or at home, he can often be spotted running on Toronto's Martin Goodman Trail.

About the Illustrator

Gordon Bagshaw, a stay-at-home dog parent of two beautiful shelties, is also a Canadian author and freelance illustrator. He loves to work with digital art, CG model texture painting, vector drawing, and bitmap painting. He is the creator of the online comic strip, *Frodo the Sheltie*, including three book galleries and illustrator of the children's book, *Sleepy Time For Mammals*, which garnered 1 of 3 L.M. Montgomery Literature for Children Awards in 2014. Gordon has resided in São Paulo, Brazil since 2008 with his lovely wife, where he teaches English for business, travel, and continued education.

Thank you for reading!

If you liked this book, you may like some of our other titles.

Who We Are...

Mirror World Publishing is a small, independent publishing house based in Windsor, Ontario. We publish quality paperbacks and e-books that feature other worlds, times and versions of reality. Our novels are for all ages and are creative, unique, imaginative, and engaging.

To learn more about our authors and our current projects visit: www.mirrorworldpublishing.com or follow @MirrorWorldPub on social media.

CPSIA information can be obtained
at www.ICGtesting.com
Printed in the USA
LVRC011506040920
665027LV00005B/18

9 781987 976748